THE STATUE AT AMBATTUR

Love Never Fails, Lust Many Times

PRESANNA KUMAR R

ISBN-13: 9798860083844
ISBN-10: 1477123456

Cover design by: Art Painter
Library of Congress Control Number: 2018675309
Printed in the United States of America

*DEDICATED TO MY PARENTS WHO KINDLED
THE SPIRIT BEHIND THIS WORK.*

Athul was an IT professional in Cognizant. His first appointment was at Coimbatore and later promoted and transferred to Ambattur, Chennai, India. He was familiar with that place in his childhood days and he has so many cherished memories with Ambattur. As an adolescent youth of 20 years, he became acquainted with a beautiful lady Sakuntalacca. To him, it was deep love, his first charming for a lady.

When he was again in Ambattur as part of the transfer, he was in total confusion. To have a solution, his wife Shalini quit her job and they shifted to Perambalur with their children and mother. Perambalur was a middle place to Chennai and they had an ancestral home there. He regularly traveled in buses to the IT hub at Ambattur.

On the first salary day here, as a gratitude, he planned a visit to Ambattur where Athul's distant sister was residing. He recollects his adolescent love affair and is eager to know the heroine in the love story.

This story illustrates adolescent behavior patterns and their findings. The end of the passional experience was heart-piercing and a warning to society.

The story is again woven around Tamil Nadu and the rich culture of that state. Actually, the story has got link to Kerala, the Palaghat, and traditional Nair Tharavads. It states the migration of border state people in search of education, jobs, and of course life.

The great flow of human generation never ceases and it will be aggressive as time passes.

India is a vast country with different tastes, but they mingle for one main cause, to lead a life. For that, all borders will be kept broken and access are free to enjoy.

This is the beauty of India.

TO ALL LOVERS OF THE WORLD.

PREFACE

To love someone is nothing, to be loved by someone is something, to love someone who loves you is everything - Bill Russel

The best love quotes are those that nail our feelings in one memorable sentence.

Passionate love is shown in infatuation as well as the most speculation on the phenomenon of love. In the present century, the science of psychology has narrated a great deal on the divine subject.

What is the most aspect of a lasting love affair?

1. TRUST
2. COMMUNICATION
3. PASSION
4. COMPATIBILITY

Two major Sanskrit epic of Ancient India revered in Hinduism are Mahabharata and Ramayana.

The first and foremost love story was Lord Krishna's affair with Gopi Radha. Vedas even does't mention about the Gopi Radha. instead kept mum.

We can find other interesting pairs in these epics:-

1. Arjuna and Ulupi
2. Ganga and Shantanu
3. Bhima and Hidimbi
4. Pandavas and Draupadi

These are only tip of an iceberg. These epics denotes bhakthi movements, but it also projects the human feelings in a new arena.

Ramayana is the full life history of Srirama and his voyage. His intense love for Sitadevi as well as the hurdles he had to suffer in safe guarding her was thrilling the generations irrespective of age.

Love may be blind, binding, piercing, lustful, one sided, winning and of course failure.

But we may be in love, knowingly or not, none can escape out of it. This is the general law of human race everwhere in the world.

"I love you for all that you are, all that you have been and all that you will be" -Unknown.

What is the difference between "I like you" and "I love you"?

It is beautifully answered by Gautama Buddha :

"When you like a flower, you just pluck it. But when you love a flower, you water it daily. One who understand this, understand life."

PREFACE

The Statue at *Ambattur*[1] is a story about an IT professional and his adolescent love affair. He in a later stage married another IT professional and they lived happily with two kids. But, the lady that sparked first love in his heart never vanished, but flashed again when he got an occasion after twenty five years.

The kick for writing this book was from a scene on the way to bus stand at Perambalur in Tamil Nadu, a state of India. Near the bus stand there was a mountain of garbage, rotten and foul smelling with so many animals and birds struggling for food. In the center, there was a human being, may be lunatic, searching for food calmly without scolding with his rivals, eats with delight a packet of damn mixture.

He was staying in Tamil Nadu, in a flat that was on rent. The place, the calmness of the village, the vividly colored flock and the tightly packed residential areas provided huge amounts of resources to write. Naturally it may be reflected in his narration but he had refurnished it to tune with fiction.

The adolescent period description was the result of author's stay at Chennai during his college days. His updation about Ambattur city was from his personal experience there after thirty years.

He opined that the twins picturized here was picked up from the *Kodambakkam*[2] Railway colony, very near to his stay. His stay at Chennai at various periods were the motivation to characterise the various persons in fictious level. To cut short, the places of visit were minimised in number and description.

The IT sector is said to be the fast growing and most dynamic industry in the world. Computers have become essential to everyone's life and are used in every industry. Education, communication, business, entertainment, construction, medicine, defense are some of the various fields computer reigns.

His main character Athul, was a skilled IT professional and his wife Shalini, another IT professional, represents the modern youth of flourishing India. Like the modern era youth who weave dreams around this industry clearly and firmly represents the present day scenario.

The average salary for IT professional is Rs. 8,55,523 per year in India. The highest salary for an IT professional in India is Rs. 15,07,871 per year. Also, the lowest salary for an IT professional in India is Rs. 3,45,944 per year.

Anyway, it is glamourous profession indeed.

The author concentrate more on the peripheral field of IT professionals, their family life, frustrations, feelings, love affairs that happened in various stages of life, failures and melancholy.

He with determination stated that he will peep into the IT professional life in a fictious approach without delay. His vision about that field can be projected and the perspiration of the elited class should be exposed in future.

This story is weaved around the expectations and outcomes of Indian reality.

His first kindle publication, "Grand Old Lady @ Rooftop Room" was a good narration of the intense love of a son to his mother.

This is his second kindle publication and I am sure it will be accepted by the mass.

USHUS

THE STATUE AT AMBATTUR

I am an IT professional working at COGNIZANT[3] in Chennai. Formerly I was at Coimbatore Cognizant as my first appointment. Though I live in this village, near Perambalur, with a lot of tamarind trees and neem trees, I was forced to join the company as it gives me and my family a reasonable shelter. We are from Coimbatore, called Manchester in India. Coimbatore was my father's native place and he has no assets there. All the properties were given to his sisters in connection with their marriage. We moved to Perambalur in Tamil Nadu, which was located in the central part of the state. It was bifurcated from Tiruchirappalli district in 1995. Here, my mother had some properties including an old house given by her father and we started life here after my father's death. I was at the age of forty-five then.

Perambalur was a developing district, and so beautiful hamlets still flourish there. We get a glimpse of the 11th-century Buddha statues in and around the villages. They are called Perambalur Buddhas.[4]

It is 267 km from Chennai. But I have no choice but to live in this place. Here in my family, I have a wife and two children. Plus, my aged mother depends solely on me. I am their only son.

I used to travel by bus for 3 hours every day to reach Chennai. Chennai is a metropolis in South India. It is vast and diverse. Chennai with its slums, street vendors, movie stars, and their palatial homes, the dramas of political liberators are mated together. Being part of the Deccan plateau, the city continues to expand very widely. Stretched out the legs like a prostitute, chewing betel nut leaves and spitting, those who come and go are easily welcomed. It is true that cities don't always sleep, never hide emotions, and never listen to or bother. It runs fast without interruptions or emotions because it is heartless and difficult to break. No one can predict what will happen in the next moment.

The morning breeze annoys me a lot. The bus is moving at a high speed. The journey from the less crowded countryside to the city streets is from natural beauty to madness. In fact, I have received many offers from other IT companies and I have participated in many interviews. But I stick to this elementary company. I don't know the exact reason. But one thing I need to mention is that I love my company and its environment. Not an increase in benefits, but the peace and tranquility I need.

I reached Ambattur where my IT firm is situated. Ambattur is an industrial area and a busy town.

Ambattur awakens in my mind different thoughts and sorrows. What comes to my mind is the old rural immaculacy. The newly sprouted Ambattur reveals the old face of that village in my college days. It pours sweetness and sourness to me like a virgin alike.

After my degree with my elder sister's son Aravind, I went to Chennai by local train in the second-class general compartment. It was my first long trip experience on a train since I had my education in my native place only until then. Without informing the sister, who is only my cousin, not the direct sister, I went with Aravind. To Aravind, he is going to his home and nothing happens, whether informed or not.

The train journey was so painful that there was no breathing place to have some fresh air. People of different walks and tastes mingled in a confined area and created all kinds of troubles on the train. Some people with more ingenuity and overenthusiasm climbed the luggage rack at the top and started their sleep after replacing the luggage. This is a general compartment and hence there is no reservation, berth, etc. Anyone can enter this type of compartment having a valid ticket and there is no gender discrimination. Beggars, Coolies after their toil, and fish-selling fisherwomen with big aluminum dishes full of fish having foul smells also ply in this cheap mode of transport in India.

This is India, with different cultures, creeds, and religions. Unity in Diversity is the country's motto. So, like different types of animals in the deep forest, everyone mingles, quarrels, and enjoys the life they have left with. This train is a replica of the outer world.

After passing behind so many stations we finally reached Egmore railway station. It is just adjacent to Chennai Central Station. Chennai is a big station and crowded always. To reduce the workload, the Indian Railway raised the adjacent stations to a higher level and accommodated some trains from each side.

From Egmore we have to pick electric trains which are plying on multiple tracks on five minutes intervals. It is my first experience with an electric train and now it is a common phenomenon everywhere in India. Its running thrilled me because there is no smoke or unnecessary tilting. On a smooth track, I felt I was in a feather touch enjoyment. We alighted at Kodambakkam railway station to go to Aravind's ancestral house which is just opposite the station. For that, we have to cross the tracks to the opposite side. We climbed the high-raised pavements made up of concrete slabs crossed the tracks to the opposite part and stepped down to the adjacent bitumen road. It was so hotter that my feet felt the heat even though I was using a chappal.

The movement of Aravind was so swift that I perspired to reach with his pace. He was so thrilled to see his parents and grandparents. Now he had reached the first phase of his journey. He reached the large Chennai city where his relatives were living scattered. He is living and studying in Coimbatore by staying with his grandma and grandpa. He along with his uncle of the same age and me are studying in Ramakrishna Educational Institutions, near Choolaimedu in the same class from the first standard onwards. On vacations, he returns to his home in Chennai. This time, I also accompanied as said earlier.

He went straight to his home and opened the closed door without any intimation. But I felt a little nervous since it was the first time I was here. Even though they were familiar to me, I felt the fault I had committed. My parents must first inform them that I am also coming with Aravind this time for a vacation here. But that doesn't happen and now I am standing in front of this house in a dilemma. He disappeared to his house and I stood like a statue on the outside steps of that tiled old house.

After a few minutes later Aravind's grandma came out of the house and requested me to come in. I entered the house and saw his grandpa eating something beside the dining table. Both the grandpa and grandma are familiar to me and they stayed in my house for many days on a vacation at Coimbatore.[5] So, I got some relief this time. After ablutions, we sat near the dining table to have breakfast. Since it was an abrupt visit breakfast was shared.

My uncle was staying in this vast compound comprising more than one acre, just opposite to Kodambakkam railway station. It was worth crores and crores and it solely belonged to Dr. K.P. Menon. He belonged to Kollengode of Palghat, Kerala. When he completed his M.B.B.S. from Madras Medical College of Tamil Nadu Govt., he started his practice in this place as a small hospital. It flourished so that he forgot to return to his native place or to have a marriage in his life. He belonged to the Kollengode Thazhattu Nair Joint Family and he was the Karnavar. All his sisters, their sons and daughters, his younger brothers, and their sons and daughters came with him to Chennai and he made a big posh house there at that time. He purchased the barren lands adjacent to his hospital and it became a large plot. At that time people of the common flock relied on quack doctors and got cheated.

He observed the pathetic condition of old Tamil Nadu and decided to treat them, the downtrodden with compassion, not with greed to earn. He became famous for his charity and he was well-recognized by the general public. For his achievement, the people with deep love renamed the road adjacent to his compound as Dr.K.P.Nair Road even when he was alive and active.

At that time, the Chief Minister of Tamil Nadu was Dr. M.G. Ramachandran [6], who is also from Palghat and he gave Dr.K.P.Nair some awards for his humanitarian works. He allotted him a primary school up to the seventh standard for his concern for street dwellers and slum dwellers, poor laborer's children. He admitted students of all walks and taught those who failed to pay fees. Really, he was a role model in society at that time. In the olden days people do charity for their inner rejoice, not for show, not for money making. Now charity is a big business.

I got stomach pain due to having food from a nearby restaurant, I ate poori and masala [7] from there when I was alone for an evening walk around Kodambakkam junction. But this food retaliated by strong pain and loose motion. Instead of consulting with Dr. K.P. Nair uncle, commonly called Doctor maman[8], I requested Aravind to meet him and bring the medicines.

But the plan failed in the first phase itself. Doctor maman with a thorough examination and seeing the pale color in Aravind's eyes, suspected it may be due to jaundice. He asked Aravind to bring his urine in a small bottle given to him. Aravind revealed the truth. He scolded him for duplication and asked him to bring me.

I went to his consulting room where so many patients were gathered. He was lying in a slanting chair and enquired about my mother mentioning her name and of course about my complaint. I explained what had happened actually.

He smiled loudly and asked about my study. He instructed me not to take food from outside. In Tamil Nadu, the oil used for cooking was mustard oil and in Kerala, especially for Keralites, it was coconut oil. So, abstain from taking food outside for the first time.

He gave me some mild medicines and wished me good luck.

For the first time, I am seeing this great man. He was so simple that he never scolded me, only with compassion approached and made me a friend of his by asking about my mother. Then he enquired and prescribed medicines.

When I stood up from the stool kept near him for patients, I noticed one thing. He has no right leg and the left toe was bandaged heavily.

I looked at his face with confusion and a little pain stepped into my face. I tried to hide the feeling and returned to Aravind's home.

It was Aravind who explained the cause of my confusion about Doctor maman. His right leg was amputated from the top and his left leg was nearing the same fate. He was an acute diabetic patient. So, his distant relative Parthasarathy was appointed as his supporting aid.

God is funny, He gives and takes mercilessly. He doesn't care about the person's character, good deeds, and evil. He simply chops when the time arrives. He may be blind in judgment. But the punishment and suffering occur without the knowledge and consent of human beings. They are mere toys in the hands of the mighty God.

His medicine was mainly a laxative and I was forced to visit the toilet so many times. I was very reluctant to visit that type of open toilet, without any doors and entrance in a 90-degree angled wall to get privacy, which was cleaned by a scavenger daily in the morning. It was the usual practice of people at that time to use public places instead of a latrine, i.e., open fields, river beds, roadside, and even on the railway track.

Since he is a doctor, he constructed a long open shed with a raised platform to sit for many people at a time and a long channel below to collect the excreta. Ladies were given a separate division of the same type adjacent to it.

The large compound housed about fifty people and it was the only toilet complex. All the people visit the toilet before nine in the morning and after that scavenger couple arrives with big iron buckets and brooms. The lady scavenger cleans her section for ladies while her male partner cleans the men's toilet. They come out with iron buckets filled with human excreta on their head and the broom will be placed over it just like a cross. They visit every kitchen side of the houses to get tips. Sometimes the generous housewife provides them with a part of the breakfast, and they eat it with rejoice while standing in that same posture. If they get food in large quantities, they wrap it in a cloth bundle.

When an emergency occurs during cleaning, it will be used, and the scavenger clean that fresh part too. I have faced such an emergency and I was forced to use it while cleaning. I saw the cleaning method and it was marked in my heart. He just uses his bare hand to handle the excreta and cleans the channel with sufficient water. He then cleans his hand and wipes on his shabby cloth.

It was a strange experience for me, and it reminded me of the economic imbalance of the society. After all, they are all human beings, but poverty and illiteracy forced them to do so.

I went to my uncle's house just adjacent to Aravind's house. I with determination entered the house because it was my uncle's house. He is a railway superintendent at Chennai central office. He was busily dressing for his duty. But he warmly welcomed me in spite of little time to spend with me. He assured me to meet in the evening after duty time. He's been like that for a long time. He was strict in life as well as in office. My uncle's wife, i.e., my aunt gave me some snacks and warm tea. I gave a sack full of Kilichundan [9] mangos which were plucked from our compound. My parents exclusively packed it and instructed me to hand it to my uncle. I without any further thought did what was instructed.

Again, I went to Aravind's house after a gap of one hour and found that Aravind was going to his house in Ambattur. I don't know what happened in the background and I was also forced to accompany him. At that time, there were no trains to Ambattur and we had to go there by bus. The bus was unattractive and the conductor was an old man having a mustache. He without ringing the bell with a long string, only commands to stop and proceed by whistling and saying RIGHT as loudly as he can. Almost of the time he used the steps to do the duty, not sitting on his marked seat near the door. When the bus stops at a point, he runs to the back door or to the front door accordingly to handle the passengers. It was an amazing one-man show indeed.

On the driver's side, he was a youth, with hair style modified in tune with Sivaji Ganesan [10], the famous star of Tamil Cinema. In front of his seat, a family photo is placed, side by side with Lord Ganesha or Pillayar in Tamil, who provides an objection-free journey. The family photo is a statutory rule on the part of the driver. The family photo always remembers his beautiful family while driving, and thus accidents can be minimized by avoiding rash driving. He wrapped a yellow shall around his neck, inside the collar of his khaki uniform as it is a practice in certain workers to avoid damage due to perspiration. He sometimes sang melodious Tamil songs, especially of T. M. Soundararajan [11].

Finally, we reached Ambattur. I was stunned to see the place since it was totally a barren place with limited thatched shops at the bus stop. The bus immediately took a U-turn and escaped from the scene. But I have no other option, just follow Aravind like a goat following the group.

The way led to a small residential area with muddy roads and red soil particles purposefully sticking to our feet. All the houses are not of any posh type as in Chennai city or in Coimbatore city. This reminded the interior of Coimbatore City.

Maybe this is also an interior of Chennai and it is in the developing stage. To see this sprouting place and to live here, I have traveled a lot. For Aravind it is his heaven, it is his residence. Own residence is greater than heaven.

Here also, the same dilemma repeated. I was here without any prior intimation. Even though I was treated well here and stayed for a week, I was annoyed due to some pertinent crisis. Like Damocles [12] sword, two main questions stared at me.

I came to this house with an empty hand in spite of I had handed over a sack full of mangos that were brought from my house to my uncle only as directed by my parents. I must open the sack and share the mangos with my uncle, Aravind's grandpa, and finally to this house where my sister was residing.

Secondly, I must have to stay with my uncle who promised to meet me in the evening. Without intimating aunt, I have eloped with Aravind as he is a friend also.

These faults were the result of my lack of acquaintance with the world. I was brought up in a shell and I liked the four walls of it to an extent. I abstained from every opportunity to have an association. The first and foremost necessity of me is to stay closed in the room and have some storybooks to mingle with.

I overheard their talk in the backyard about my deed with the mangos and they mocked me after discussing my inexperience in handling a situation. Totally I felt confused and dejected. I wished to leave the place as soon as possible and reach my own home.

But at noon, when meals were served, we all took seats around a round dining table and talked freely. This was the beginning of the melting of the ice. Gradually I also became a link in that chain. I gradually began to enjoy the new environment. All the anomalies occurred due to my own fault and in a way my parents are also to an extent responsible. They must have informed me all about the matters and trained me to consider all others equally.

The vacation at Ambattur was remarkable and memorable. It was a small hamlet near Avadi, 22 km from Chennai railway station. Actually, it was a rich agricultural area comprising paddy and sugarcane. But Avadi is famous for defense factories such as Heavy Vehicles Factory and Ordnance Factory Board. Aravind's residence is a part of a plot divided into 5 cents each and several buildings were sprouting there. It was very near to the famous Avadi Maidan where Congress Annual Meet was held in the period 10th January 1955 presided by Mr. Jawaharlal Nehru, then Prime Minister of India.

Our first visit was to that maidan just behind Aravind's residence. It was only a walkable distance and we with great spirit entered the maidan through the border where palm trees were planted in a line. Numerous cattle were grazing the thickly grown grasses. Some boys are playing football in the middle of Maidan where grass growth is rare. It was a large ground comprising more than ten acres. Palm trees bordered the maidan as a fortress and the Deccan wind blew there with palm leaves vibration, just like trumpets. Nature was there in fury since defense factories were very near or just adjacent to it.

When the Sun reached the west horizon, it radiated red rays and colored the background more terribly. We left the maidan since it was going to be vacuumed after a few cattle and some boys.

The next day, after breakfast which was nice and a little heavy, went on a cycle to the nearby Redhill Lake or Puzhal Lake. It was a rainwater reservoir in the mighty city of Chennai. We had to cover a distance of more than 5 kilometers to that lake and as kids, we were least bothered about the strain and perspiration. Finally, we saw the lake at a distance of half a kilometer and we were more thrilled having the glittering site of water in the sun. It was a steep drive leaning to the lake and we with uncontrollable speed due to overweight landed in the banks of the lake itself. Luckily there was enough sand bed to stop us, otherwise, we would have fallen into the depths of that lake.

This lake is called Sengundram in Tamil meaning Red Hills. It has a past history leading to the British era. The first Transport Railway in India was started here, as Red Hill Railway to transport granite for road building in the year 1832.

We spent about two hours there walking here and there. That was a barren place at that time. Palms were scattered here and there around the lake. Only some fishermen with their country-made hooks are seriously indulged in fishing. Their baskets made of bamboo were almost full of caught fish which was struggling to escape from it. They might have started their job in the early hours of the morning. They were black in color, with scattered hair and shabby bermuda shorts. Always chewing something, they seemed to be intoxicated nature since the smell of arrack was clear when we approached them to have a close look. Their look and talk kindled in us some fear that we, quickly escaped from the scene. We are only youths of about 20 years and the arena was deserted. There was ample scope to immerse us in water and kill to have something worthy if they felt.

We were tired so that on the return trip we stopped near a man selling palm juice. It was filled in a pot made up of palm leaves well stitched with palm fiber. It was actually a mixture of palm fruits with palm toddy. It was so sweet and delicious that we brought another pot also and this nectar evaded our tiredness.

But, on the way, we felt a little dizzy since it was our first experience with toddy. We found it very difficult to drive the cycle, especially to control the handle. We sat near a temple and took some rest.

Time kept its fastness and we were cautioned about the warning given by Aravind's mother. So somehow, we started our return trip and reached home. The first thing we did was to have a good bath and get refreshed. We acted to look smarter since we were hiding a serious offense.

Aravind's house was a single-story one with four rooms. A drawing room, a bedroom, adjacent to the drawing room there was a small room and a kitchen room.

From the drawing-room, there were doors leading to all adjacent rooms. To go to the kitchen, we have to pass by the small room. So, we will get privacy only in the bedroom.

Here in the small room, there was another occupant, a little aged man with gray hair, called Srinivasa Iyer, who was a proofreader in the Indian Express Newspaper. He and his beautiful young wife Shakuntala lived in that small confinement space with coordination and happiness, which was rare and difficult to attain in life.

In that small room, obviously, there was no privacy for any couples to dwell. But they rejoiced in that limited space and freely mingled with the house owner as a family member, not as a tenant.

In certain rare moments, his wife Shakuntala visits our abode, the only bedroom, and discusses news and sometimes gets seated there to see the Television. At that time Television was Doordarsan owned by the Government of India which comprises mostly Hindi programs and regional programs just like ration. The popular Tamil program at that time was Oliyum Oliyum, based on Tamil film songs.

She expresses loudly with the serials playing on television and cries and laughs without any control. She sometimes predicts the next twist in the story and destroys the viewer's spirit. When the limit was over, Aravind's mother interfered to stop her. But after a few minutes, she will be again on the wrong path. She was actually helpless to have a break indeed.

Since I am not interested in seeing the serial, I just sit there and watch what the spectators are doing while viewing the television. Truly this was the real serial. I was more interested in viewing Shakuntalacca. She made acquaintance with me and asked me to call her likewise. She was rose-colored with dimples on either side of her cheeks. She maintains her black, thick, little curly long hair and after that decorates with fresh mallika [13] flowers brought from street vendors coming daily in a cycle. She was so friendly that she even shared her college romances and her pathetic family background which forced her to marry this aged Swami as her husband. But she regained the rejoicing of wedded life even though they have no children so far. To her it was Swami and to Swami it was totally her. Both attained the peak of marriage with no issues.

But we gossiped outside about her when we were going to the market nearby to purchase meat. Aravind was very familiar to her since she had been with them for the last ten or twelve years. Swami made friends with Aravind's father on the bus and while talking, he requested Aravind's father to accommodate his family also. Since Aravind's father was so generous and peaceful in nature, he agreed. It was not for money but for humanity, he agreed after hearing Swami's story. Also, it was a boon for them, since, the family got a person's presence in the form of Shakuntala when he was in office. It will be a great help to his wife in solitude.

Shakuntalacca was in the habit of visiting the local Hanuman temple near the market. The temple was so large and dense with neem trees and flowering plants. Jasmine was the main plant well maintained there. When we enter the premises of the temple, we will be welcomed heartily with the smell of it. It will provide us with two different versions of fragrance, one filled with God's fear and the other with Romance.

It was for the second fragrance, Shakuntalacca daily attended the temple premises. There under the big Banyan tree roundabout, a man with a big black beard sat there just only to see her, just only to have a darshan of her, and just only to have a bit of talk or for a glimpse of a smile on her reddish cheeks shaded with shyness.

Aravind's talk ceased as we entered the busy Ambattur market. We, without wasting any time went straight to the meat section at the west corner, very near to the Hanuman [14] temple. The whole premises appeared to be rubbish and foul-smelling.

Meat and its waste were placed side by side and occasionally some crows were trying to pick up the meat pieces by attacking the consumable meat itself. Crows also don't need meat waste.

There was no irregularity in keeping meat and fish near the temple. It was inside the temple it was banned. Anyway, I felt uneasiness in this behavior, especially a stream of blood that was flowing by the side of the temple wall touching and marking reddish brown color and odor. Men are selfish, more selfish when they are blind with greed.

When I sat behind the dining table having meat curry as a main dish for dinner, my mind was loitering around the unhealthy situations around the market and the crow, pulling meat, which was hung on a rusted hook on a bamboo bar and crow sitting on it as a perch, lavishly excreting.

Here also, I tried to be a spectator again, as if it is a serial. But I was caught red-handed by Shakuntalacca, who had an eye on me as a silent server since she was Brahmin and a vegetarian but liked to serve without any hesitation.

"Athul,neengal   yean   iraichi   saappidavillai? Neengal iruvarum kaalaiyil santhaiyil irunthu kondu vanthirukkireerkal. Athai muzhumaiyaaga saappidungal." 15

Shakuntalacca said in a single tenure and continued to observe my next step. I with half heart, finished the meat. But in vain, she poured the dish again without my consent. I looked at her, she was also on me, but with a mysterious smile. Why there was a mysterious smile launched on her beautiful face, like sunlight on a lotus flower? Mystery always blossoms as a smile, for women especially.

On the next day, we went to see a nearby makeshift tarpaulin tent. It was a touring talkie where three different shows were screened on a single ticket with ten-minute intervals on a single day. It was made on a paddy field after harvest without any chairs. All have to share the muddy ground with the tip of harvested paddy plants. Sometimes it may penetrate into our buttocks and make them painful. But to witness the films was a thrilling experience at that time. The first was a Tamil movie by Nadikar Thilakam Sivaji Ganesan called Sivakamyin Selvan, a remake of the Hindi film Aaradhana of Hindi Super Star Rajesh Khanna. Next was Karnan, starred again by Nadikar Thilakam Sivaji Ganesan in Tamil. The story was from the famous epic, Mahabharatha. The last film which was also in Tamil, belonged Makkal Thilakam M.G. Ramachandran called Rikshakkaran, or the Cart puller. During intervals we ate some nuts from outside and from inside there was the distribution of various eatables by small boys plying in between spectators. It was a remarkable experience even in this new era.

On the next day, I left for Chennai city with Aravind as an escort, where my uncle and aunt were residing. They welcomed me with multiple reactions and scolded me about my trip to Ambattur without intimating them. Aravind stood by my side without any comment and with a pale smile. After some time, Aravind left for his grandpa's house which was very adjacent. There were no borders, no walls, only in a single compound all the houses were constructed and temporarily distributed among relatives.

As instructed by my uncle, I resided with him for a few weeks. He asked Aravind to take me to visit the Moore market, Merina Beach, Zoo and Museum [16], and other important places to visit. One day while walking on the broad way of Kodambakkam, with Aravind, we heard film music from a studio. The name was carved on the top arch of it and it was AVM studio [17], where a film shoot was live.

We entered the studio complex since the security was one of the neighbors of Aravind. He sanctioned with one condition, don't shout or launder here and there. We agreed with great pleasure and the film shoot was on the second studio floor. We saw there a song scene in a makeshift pond side with heroin trying to fill her pot with water. Then the hero arrives and hugs her. Her earthen pot with water breaks and she shows anger to him. Then he sang a song to pacify her. It was taken in fragments and I felt no thrill in that shooting. The hero was Jayasankar and the heroine was Ushakumari. The stars are familiar to me since I have seen them in so many films.

While Aravind's grandpa took us on the electric train to the city and visited some temples. Afterward, he provided snacks and tea at the famous Woodlands Hotel. He had a season ticket to ply frequently in trains which was a common habit of old people. He regularly visits certain temples, some ashramas, and Swamiji's there. He was an ardent devotee of Saibaba of Shirdi.[18]

He knew that I was more interested in these matters than Aravind and hence always took me with him. I loved and enjoyed his divine journey and hunger for God's grace.

For this, Aravind always mocked me for accompanying his own grandpa. But he doesn't know the value of these rare and worthy moments.

It was during one such journey; that he visited The Madras Senior Citizen's Forum and registered his and his wife's name to the Funeral division of it. He later explained to me that he had done it for the children. I wondered in his statement how children would benefit from it. He, knowing my doubt, explained in detail that when he or his wife expired, he didn't want his children should suffer to take expenses or meet some agencies to perform the cremation. This was the safe outlet for a senior citizen in Chennai and it was started during the British period. He added that he was proud to be a member of that grand reputed organization and cremation after death by the same team.

His favorite menu at the Annapoorna restaurant was always masala dosa, chutney, and vada. At the end of a brisk walk to Triplicane[19], he reaches a park and chats with some same-aged members. Then he allows me to walk here and there in the park just to have some privacy for him.

I enjoyed that rare moment to the maximum to see the beauty of the park, the people, the fashionable society charms, and in total nature. The park was oval in shape comprising about three acres in the middle of the city. Large trees were grown to provide shade and coolness with turfed grass ground. Tall, Asoka pillar trees were stationed on the borders along with Palms of different colors. Red palm was the king among them.

While walking through the tiled path around the park, many evening exercisers were briskly walking in both directions. It was very difficult to walk in between them such that they may hit us during their work.

Finding the huge rush there, I sat on a bench, near a big Pine tree and started viewing the moving city stream of vivid color. It was a stream full of different colors, odors, and characters. Both fashionable and common mingled in the stream without looking at each other. All are in a hurry, doing exercises and burning their fat to be fit for life.

All the benches around were almost full of different age groups. They tried their best to gather according to their age group. To have a discussion, gossiping, and mere chatting it was a must. These bench groups have no sex discrimination, only age is the factor.

Usually, the old age group forms in male or female partitions. That shows they are still on the old path and methodology. But for the youth, it was another arena. They freely mingle and talk without any limitations. They are more rational in thoughts and deeds.

My opposite bench was occupied by youths. Maybe they are from nearby colleges, and some are hostel mates, who are spending some time here to have an escape from the boring academic syllabus. Five boys and two girls were seated on a single bench as a cluster. They are enjoying everything under the sky without looking at the passing stream. Occasionally they break the talk and look at the people passing briskly. They even commented on their movement and tried to imitate their way of walking, dressing, and way of talking.

Usually, during walking exercises, people prefer loose dresses as far as possible. Wind often causes the little dresses to fly up. Brisk movements of the body and its parts provide the charm of dancing. For the youth, irrespective of age they comment and consume the spirit with humor and little lust.

In the madding crowd, it was my nature to be a silent spectator as far as possible. I simply sit there and observe. I could see what was happening around me, feel the pulse of people, and without their attention.

I heard whispering behind my chair. It was well known to me. That sound was well acquainted. That was the talk of a lady and her sound resembled someone recently met. Who was she?

I looked back and there was nothing visible from this angle. A massive bush-type plant hides that place like a fortress. But still, I could hear that talk, a loud smile.

Grandpa was coming on the tiled path and he was in search of me. I can see him from a little distance. He had finished his rejoicing chat and joke today and tried to enter his nest before the desk, just like a bird. I stood up from the park chair and was ready to leave with him. I followed Grandpa and he was in a hurry today.

As a shortcut, he entered the meadow where the bushes are planted and tried to reach the exit gate diagonally. When we reached the bush, I just turned back. There on the hiding of bush growth, on the grass cushion, a young lady was sitting and, in her lap, a black beard man was pointing at the orange Sun, who was in the final stage today. The lady was still laughing with delight, passion, and compassion. Yes, She, was Shakuntalacca.

A flash and thunder sprouted in me. It waved in and distributed almost all parts of my body like electricity. It was a high-tension potential difference that penetrated my mind also.

On the way, I was just following with Grandpa in total

dejection and confusion. He was describing something relevant to see and it was of national importance connected with the Independence movement of India. But I was not here, only following him like a goat that was directed to slaughterhouse.

In the night, while I was in bed, sleep disappeared from the scene. Thoughts poured ice water on my head and I was behind Shakuntalacca.

Shall I reveal what I saw in the park to Aravind and release my tension to an extent?

No, it will create more trouble for her, and that I don't want to happen.

What was forcing me to be stuck on her, her beauty, her talk, her body shape, or that smile with mystery?

I don't know exactly, but I know one thing, I was bonded to her. I was a little possessive about her.

After a few stray thoughts, I was in a sleep, which was deep and filled with sweet dreams. When you are in love, all the moments appear sweet, lovely, and encouraging.

On the next day I with the permission of my aunt went to the park again in the evening alone. The way was very clear to me since I will make a new path if the situation emerges. That was my condition then. But to my bad luck, there was no trace of Shakuntalacca.

I walked a little more distance to another junction and there was another small park. I entered that park with eagerness to see her. She was not here.

How could I contact her once more?

It was the need of the hour. It was the motive behind my actions. I can't resist my mind and its directions. Just like a kite in the wind, having its control string which was broken, I flued in the mercy of airflow.

How could I contact her once more?

The next day, I returned to Ambattur with Aravind, who was going there for a short stay, I also followed with him. This time I was with a great mission and intention.

I pledged in mind that I would never reveal anything about Shakuntalacca to anyone in my life. Let it be a top secret that fixes and rests in my mind only forever.

We reached the Ambattur bus stand and I was so fast to step down. I looked around the market nearby, the Hanuman temple, and its premises. There was no trace of what I was in an intense search.

What a fool I am! She was staying in Aravind's home and we are approaching that destination soon. By keeping money in my purse, I am stretching my hands for alms.

We reached Aravind's home and his mother, who was my sister also in a way, welcomed us cordially. This time, I was here only for a short stay just to say farewell, and I wanted to return to my house in Coimbatore after visiting my aunt's house in Chennai. He had already booked a train ticket for my return journey.

But, after seeing Shakuntalacca, who was cleaning their shabby clothes in a corner, I felt a little agony to depart soon. I approached her with great passion and spirit. She was friendly to me and talked while washing clothes.

She talked about my stay at my uncle's house in Chennai. She wants to know everything about that house, uncle, aunt, their approach to me, etc.

"Sennaiyil ithuvarai neengal sendra idangal evai?" 20

I narrated all the names of important places I have visited in detail. This time I was very interested in talking with her.

"Triplicaneil   ulla   asoka   poongavukku
        sendrirukkireerkalaa?" 21

She again asked. I looked at her stunned. She had a smile while asking that particular question. Smile, that same old mysterious smile. I also smiled back, genuinely

"Unnai andha poongavil thaaththaavudan paarthirukkiren, Kanna" 22

I looked at her with a strange hunger. But she neglected my feelings and asked me to stay away from the washing point a little far to avoid water drops falling on me.

Behind the kitchen yard, there was a guava plant with ripe fruits. I waited there in the shade as if to pluck and eat the fruit. While eating, I was upon her and she was not.

I observed her beauty while she was indulged in washing. She was now waving clothes in the air, after dipping in water and striking a slanting stone. The water droplets derived lakhs of minute color dots on a sunny day and she stood in the middle of that rainbow like a goddess. Goddess, Goddess of love indeed.

To minimize the wetting of her undergarments, she fixed the bottom of it in her waist in a triangle shape, as is the common practice of Indian women. In the glittering beam, I could see her white naturality from a different angle and ambiance. To capture the sweating drops glittering in the sun, from her face, I advanced a step.

At that crucial moment, Aravind appeared at the kitchen door and called me.

"Athul, dinner is ready."

He disappeared from the scene. I with desperation plucked another guava fruit and moved slowly beside her.

Now, she looked again and smiled, but the mysterious nature was absent.

I gave that guava fruit to her with a trembling heart. She accepted and started eating it. I was quite relieved.

After dinner, I slept for a while in the bedroom under the breeze of a fan. It was a much hotter day and I felt uneasiness to lie on the foam bed. I went outside and sat under a neem tree on the front side in a wooden chair. The natural flow of the Ambattur wind made me sleepy fast.

I was later awakened by a noise. It was the sound produced by the opening of a window. The window belonged to the room where Shakuntalacca was staying. I opened my eyes with difficulty since I was still in a hangover from interrupted sleep.

She was near the window and combing her long hair after a bath. She put on face powder and kajal was applied to her eye and surrounding valleys. She wore a pink saree in the hide of the wall and again appeared near the window. She then fastened mallika garland on her hair. The fragrance was so penetrating that I stood up from the chair and went towards the window to have a close look. The fragrance intensified in close range mixed with her odor. It provoked the man in me and I placed my right hand on the window. She also placed her hand upon it. It was so hot like an oven.

"Athul"

Aravind's mother called me in. I entered the house and my snacks and tea were served there. She also said that Shakuntala was going to Chennai to meet her relatives there to attend a marriage. It was safer to have her company instead of going alone. So, prepare and dress urgently.

I was so thrilled to have a journey with her. But I never exhibited my thoughts outside. Aravind and his mother were so happy that I was not alone on the return trip to Chennai. To them, I am a newcomer and not acquainted with the nook and corner of the large Chennai metropolitan city.

We walked through the muddy roads leading to the bus stand silently. Almost all the house owners were her friends. Some people asked her, who I am and she replied with a smile that he was the brother of her house owner Saralacca. To keep a distance from me, she was keeping mum.

At the bus stand, we waited for a while to get the bus to Chennai. There was no trace of her lover and I got little happiness and relief. At last, she was with me without any hindrance.

When the bus arrived, we entered it. There was no rush inside the bus and I got a seat near the window. To my surprise and as my wish she sat near me. When the conductor asked for tickets, she brought two tickets to Chennai.

The bus moved and she with a smile started her talk. The talk pictured her true story and why she was behind that bearded man.

That man was her lover from her college days. She was a graduate of Tamil literature and was unemployed. She stopped her further education since poverty engulfed her family. So, the relatives married her to an old man at the age of 20 and got relieved. The old man, proofreader Swami needs a friend, not a wife, and it was his second marriage at the age of 54. He considered her like a child and loved her without any limits. He never distrusted her and she was given freedom in life.

I looked at her. Her eyes were filled with tears and actually fell on my left hand due to the wind flowing inside through the opposite window of the running bus. I picked up her right hand and held it tightly. It was cold like ice.

Where was the hotness now? At the window side of Aravind's home, it was hot like an oven. At what depth does the rainfall of feelings reduce the hotness to ice cubes of Insensitivity?

"Athul, nee enakku oru sagotharan pondravan."23

"Nandraaga padiththu ennai ninaivil kol"24

"Nee en thambi .. nee en thambi .."25

She held my hands in her and gently patted me with love. Now I was dipped in the avalanche of snow.

The peak of emotions was shattered, a new dawn of wisdom broke out and blossomed. Now I was in my real shoes.

At Chennai central bus stand, we parted with deep pain. I without any intention looked at her, vanishing in the crowd like a flash. I wished She may turn back once again to have a darshan, but that never happened.

With heavy hearts, I reached my uncle's home. It was too late, my uncle scolded me. It further intensified my sorrow and I kept abstaining from any food for the false reason that I was with stomach ache.

Actually, the fast was for my first love failure, and for Shakuntalacca who disappeared in thin air.

It may be an adolescent love affair. But like monkeys, this vibrant novel behavior grabs firmly on anything just opposite to natural order.

Anyway, I was in love. Now I am not.

With a firm decision, I slept calmly.

The next day, I am leaving this city on the evening train from Egmore Station. For that, I have to travel by electric train from Kodambakkam to Egmore. It was the reverse process of my previous journey from Coimbatore.

The train started in slow steps and attained pace later. But my mind was in reverse mode. I came to this city with an open heart, with much space for anything to absorb. But now it was filled with an anonymous gel. It sticks in my thoughts and deeds.

I firmly closed my eyelids and leaned back.

It was a diesel engine train and it makes long horns on turnings and at every five minutes gap. If there were no horns, the engine would be stopped suddenly thinking that there was no driver inside and he was not alert. This was the programming inside to avoid accidents due to negligence on the part of the driver. Besides the long and penetrating horns make him alert as well as evade cattle and people who are crossing or on a walk on tracks.

On the upper berth of the compartment, I put my personal belongings like a purse and watch near the small white pillow with engravings of the Indian Railway. Since it was a non-air-conditioned coach, I felt very hot on the top. I looked down to have a glimpse of co-passengers. They have already dipped in sleep and some are snoring loudly. I felt annoyance again at these snoring sounds but was helpless to abate them.

I turned to the opposite side facing the partition and tried to hug sleep firmly.

I woke up at Salem junction. People are getting off the train and getting in such that the train would leave soon. It was a major junction and here the halt interval is ten minutes. Erode junction and Tirupur are the stations left before the Coimbatore junction. So, I got down from the upper berth and prepared to get down. I took my personal belongings from the top berth and kept them intact.

The train was still held at Salem junction, which may be due to some signal issues arising with the upcoming trains. Usually, all the tracks in India were supersaturated with trains creating traffic blocks and time delays.

I stood from my seat and went towards the door. I looked at the signal of the track. It was still red. So, with confidence, I went to the nearby tea shop on the platform and ordered a hot coffee. He served it in a paper cup and I moved towards the door of the compartment. Looking at the signal, I sipped the hot coffee with delight. After finishing it, I dropped the cup in the waste bin and quickly approached the door. Now, the signal was clear. It was green indeed.

Salem junction remembers the grandpa of Aravind. His work site was here and for years he was employed here in the Sri Raam Chemical Factory as a supervisor. He was in control of the Hydrochloric Acid production unit. The factory was under Govt. of India. Since he was from Salem, he was nick-named Salem maman, or uncle from Salem.

The train moved with fast steps to cover the delayed time.

After stopping at the two stations, the train reached Coimbatore junction at the right time. Mostly Indian Railways keep Departure time and Arrival times up to the timetable as far as possible. In all other, in-between stations, it may be delayed.

In an autorickshaw, I reached my home after three weeks. I was again in the abode of my sweet home. My memories are filled everywhere on these four walls. After a lapse of time, I am here to regain and retain my dreams.

My parents looked at me as if they were seeing me for the first time. I brought them grapes and plums, which were filled in palm leaf baskets, from the Kodaikanal road station. It was garden fresh items and was famous and cheap.

After my degree result, I got a B.Tech in Computer Science from Amrita University of Coimbatore and then got employed in a local IT firm as a System Analyst. I have worked for that firm for about five years and after acquiring practical experience I applied for a job at Cognizant here.

My luck was granted by God's grace and now I have become an I.T. employee. It was my ambition to be an I.T. professional. I know that it was the way in the future world. The job at Cognizant became a turning point in my life.

I met Shalini in the corridor of Cognizant She has been working here for the past three years. I am a fresher in this company since I had pre-experience in another firm. She was my mentor in the I.T. field because I have worked previously as a system analyst.

During the entry period here, I was put under the leadership of Shalini Madam. She cleared each and every aspect of doubts arising in the course of the IT job. As a safe method, I relied on her directions frequently and got acquainted with her.

My Company was providing various IT services more than fifty seven different categories. The Cognizant company was into software and application development, consulting, business process outsourcing, payment processing, technology education services, asset leverage solutions, cloud infrastructure, enterprise solutions, etc. It also includes in-house developed software products. It ventured into application development , complex systems integration and consulting work. Cognizant had a period of fast growth during the 2000s , becoming a Fortune 500 company in 2011. In 2015, the Fortune magazine named it as the world's fourth most admired IT services company. It is headquartered in Teaneck, New Jersey, U.S. Cognizant is part of the NASDAQ-100 and trades under CTSH.

I was put under the leadership of one Shalini Madam during the entry period. She cleared each and every aspect of doubts arising in the course of the IT job.

Shalini Madam got a beautiful smile which I noted in the initial stage itself. When I saw her, very close, at a laptop distance, handling the same keyboard and mouse, sharing the same cubicle, air, and of course the same snacks and tiffin, we met each other. Our faces came so close that we breathed the same moment in resonance.

I never asked her religion, instead loved her.

I never asked her caste, of course, instead loved firmly.

I looked at her beauty, efficiency, and fluency in talk, especially in English which was a must in the IT profession.

Our marriage was solemnized in a short time in the local Mahalekshmi Kalyana Mandapam and all the IT friends participated. She was welcomed to my house with great rejoicing by my parents and relatives.

On the first night, we talked about our personal tastes. It was so similar that we could synchronize easily for a better married life. After a few stray talks, I put off the light.

Shalini Madam vanished and Shalini was born again in the darkness, without any compulsion or complaint.

Our life streamed through the valleys and rocky areas with the same pace, music, and surf. Valleys adorned in due course with charming flowers and we enjoyed the married life as a symphony.

We became parents of two children, Swagath and Swetha, the twins of our dreams. They were so identical that they ate, thought, acted, and dressed in the same pitch. They became the talk of the surrounding colony because of their similarity.

Life went uninterrupted and one day that happened. My ailing father died in the bathroom due to a massive heart attack. Our family was immersed in deep grief because our father was the prime attraction and charm of our family. His absence tilted my mother for a certain period and she picked up momentum in due course by mingling with our children, Swagath and Swetha.

A maidservant was appointed to assist the mother in the kitchen and to have a friend in need when we were away in the Cognizant. Chinnamma as was called by my mother usually finishes her household duties and sits in the drawing room. She was addicted to two things, one chewing betel leaves, the other viewing television programs. She sits on the floor cross-legged for hours in the same posture as in a yoga pose. She was black in color, bulky with huge buttocks and it oscillated on her walk, like a pendulum on either side.

The first thing my wife did was to make Chinnamma tidy. She gave a new blade to her and asked to cut short her fingernails, where so much dirt was hiding. She was asked to clean her hands daily with soap and water before entering the kitchen.

Chinnamma was funnier and she entered the kitchen after a full bath in the bathroom outside. Then she fastened mallika flowers to have an odor and made food. She served food with taste and fragrance. Now, there was dance and fragrance in her body and taste in her hand.

The very next year I was promoted as CEO of a Cognizant division but transferred to Chennai. From HR, I came to know that I was posted at the Ambattur Cognizant. I felt a little annoyed but there was no other way, just to suffer and join the division. For some relief, I went to the toilet by the side of the HR room.

Ambattur, after almost twenty-five years I am going to that place. I looked at the mirror near the wash basin. There I can see two figures, an adolescent boy of twenty years and the other a charming lady, Shakuntalacca.

We discussed the issue caused by the transfer in the family and finally, we reached a possible conclusion. Either I or Shalini must resign to keep the family and we must shift to our mother's house at Perambalur. I approached my mother and consulted. She was double okay since, after long days she was going to her native place, her sweet home, and the familiar surroundings.

The project was executed. The only resistance from my children was that they would miss school, friends, and teachers. But they also cooperated in the end.

At first, the family suffered a lot to adjust to my salary even though it was raised almost to thirteen lakhs per annum, the loss of Shaliini's salary was prominent on some occasions. But Shalini with her management skill tackled the situations amazingly.

She with the help of skilled laborers started vegetable farming in the five-acre field which was the unattended property of my mother. Also, with the help of experts and their advice, introduced the drip irrigation method and kept vigil on the farm.

Our maidservant Chinnamma was very helpful in Shalini's farming and she frequently visited the farm which was very adjacent to our house. Not in beauty, but in duty one should be estimated.

I appreciated and encouraged Shalini since she would be rusted if kept idle in the home. Iron brittles only when it was used. An idle mind is a devil's workshop, especially of a lady.

Shalini adjusted the time schedule in tune with the family members, especially with children. Their study, school, and any other crisis would be tackled promptly and neatly.

At first, Shalini was a little desperate without a job. It was a normal situation, that when we lose a job, it will be more piercing. She kept silent for the first few weeks and later picked up.

For me, it was very heartbreaking to be alone in the firm, after having worked in pairs. In the new venue, I was so gloomy in the first week that colleagues asked about the reason. I replied with a smile to everyone.

I got my first salary from here today and decided to visit Aravind's home. Actually, I had forgotten to visit them on the first day itself. If I visit them, they will request me to stay there for a day at least. So, I mentioned the matter to my wife in the morning itself. She was okay to handle the vacuum.

After twenty-five years I am walking towards the remote corner of Ambattur. The bus stand, temple, and market were still intact, but with new faces and development.

The bus stand was widened and concreted. A new building and shopping complex were attached to it. The Hanuman temple with huge trees was welcoming devotees as earlier. A compound wall was made to the temple. On the branches, there are numerous monkeys playing and asking devotees for food. They even appear on the compound wall and jump outside. They can be seen in the bus stand also. Devotees offer food and water to them. They resemble and represent the God Hanuman.

The market was modernized with stalls and drainage. The fish and meat waste were stored in concrete tanks and fermented to manure. The thick smell of rotten flesh and blood vanished to an extent.

But something was missing in the background. What was it?

I walked on the stretched road, but the road was tarred and had a modern outlook. The old muddy road was replaced by time. So many high-rise flats emerged after demolishing the old houses. In my mind, I have only the direction. The old house was near the Avadi maidan. I walked towards the maidan and finally reached my destination.

The old house was renovated and reconstructed into a double-storied one. The whole area was totally changed and I was confused about the status of this house.

I pressed the calling bell and waited outside with little doubt. The door was opened and my confusion was over. Saralacca was there to welcome me.

"Athul, how many years have I seen you? Have you been here for any other purpose?"

Aravind's mother, my distant sister, asked in a nonstop step. I smiled and entered the house as the old adolescent child.

At the dining table, we sat face to face and narrated my story. After hearing that I was employed here at Cognizant, she insisted on staying.

She talked about her family and the changes that happened. Her husband Ramettan, an LIC[26] section head of Mount Road [27]Head office, died after his retirement. She was now alone here and the upstairs was given on rental. Aravind was at Kodambakkam with his family and doing some business there. On some occasions, she visits his son Aravind and stays there for a week. But she was more comfortable here since she could light an oil lamp on the remains of her husband kept near the jack tree, which was planted by him.

Almost all Indian women, after marriage clings to her husband, his physical, his mental, and after death, his memory. This was the normal cycle of good Indian women.

I looked at my sister, she was not now my distant sister, sister itself. She looked aged with gray hair and a little tired.

I walked around the renovated house and found it up to date. She also accompanied me with difficulty and said –

Ramettan's retirement amount was spent here to renovate it. He lived in this new house for almost six years and died in the hospital. At first Aravind with his family lived with me and for business, he had to leave me.

Two bedrooms, one drawing cum dining room, and a modular kitchen were on the ground floor. The same pattern was repeated on the first floor.

Again, we reached the dining area and sat there to continue talking. She was alone here for a long time and eager to have a talk, especially to discuss family matters.

During the talk, I remembered the missing factor that I felt at the Ambattur bus stand.

Shakuntalacca, the beautiful young wife of an old man. Where was She?

While hiding my personal interest, I casually recalled her name and about her husband, the proofreader Swami.

"Saralacca, where is Shakuntalacca and her husband?"

She without any interest replied that Shakuntala had left

31

the house after purchasing an old house nearby and started living there.

Saralacca stopped the discussion and went to the kitchen. She came with a Chirag, placed it on a stone near the jack tree, and prayed for a while with closed eyes.

She then went to the prayer corner and chanted divine mantras loudly. I with folded hands prayed standing behind her and got outside.

The sky was reddish in color. Birds are flying in flocks to their nest in arrow shape.

I searched for the neem tree. No, it was already chopped down. From here, I witnessed Shakuntalacca near the rear of her bedroom window, I touched her hands as if a desert storm.

Now the window was there, with a new edition, but no trace of Shakuntalacca.

Where was she now? What happened to that small family?

I went to the back side of the house. The old washing stone was there and it had a canopy of a new neem tree. The guava plant was not there, instead, replaced with a coconut plant. The water from the washing point was channeled to its pit.

I still remember the happy moments under the guava. It was here that I loved and showed interest in her. I gave them a guava fruit and she ate it without any hesitation.

In the glittering Sun, her natural beauty made me a slave to her. I felt the same shivering of adolescent feelings and intense lust here, in this reddish arena of the desk.

I am now a father with a beautiful wife and two children, but still, the passion for Shakuntalacca is still alive and firing in me.

I quickly returned to the front and met Saralacca. She was in search of me after finishing the prayer. I washed my legs and hands and entered the house.

I was provided the small bedroom which was formerly of Shakuntalacca and Swami. But it was reconstructed, avoiding the common passage to the kitchen. The kitchen was provided with a new corridor.

During supper, chapati and dal curry were served. I again mentioned Swami and Shakuntalacca .

This time she picked my bite and answered. It was a long tale and she took almost one hour to complete it.

I had already said earlier that Shakuntala bought an old house nearby and they shifted to it from our house. It was this shift that caused all the tragedy.

The story was woven around her bearded lover and her tarnished image due to her illicit relationship with him. In due course, she conceived a baby and delivered it at the Kilpauk Medical College[28], Chennai. The male child was treated as his son by age-old Swami and accepted in the heart as raindrops in the desert. Shakuntala nurtured the boy in a way that there was ample freedom and concern for him. He attained the age of five and was admitted to the school. The school was just opposite Avadi Maidan and he had to cross the Maidan as a shortcut. Since her child was only five years old, she accompanied him in the initial days. Gradually she stopped that habit since the boy got so many friends and they enjoyed freedom by going without parental support.

Swami was a little afraid of this new system and he requested her to follow him up to the Maidan border. Behind the palm trees, she waits in hiding and returns after her child disappears into the group.

This was followed for many days and they were happy with the child. But one ill lucky evening, the boy was missed. She mourned loudly and neighbors searched the entire maidan. At last, the boy was found dead in a bush, near a wild fruit plant. He had been there to pluck the fruits and that bush was rich with poisonous snakes. At the hospital, the doctor identified the same cause.

Swami was more hurt than Shakuntala since the boy was a great relief to him after his boring proofreading work. He lamented for several days and finally concentrated on his work. But to Shakuntala, it can't be forgotten easily.

They wept for many nights and finally decided to make a statue of their child in front of their house in the mini garden. The statue was the size of a five-year-old boy and the face resembled almost their child. A mandap was created exclusively for the statue and Shakuntala began to sit there looking at the child's face while swami was in office. She will sit leaning on a pillar of mandap facing her boy's statue and read devotional books or chant hymns. Sometimes she sleeps there at the foot of the statue. On such occasions, she may forget to bathe or perform sandhya vandhanam[29]. She will be there until called by her husband who was coming from the office. Both of them enter their home with heavy hearts and slow paces.

With great curiosity, I looked at my sister and asked about the final stage. The time was nine-thirty now and She appeared to be sleepy. I was afraid that she may stop today and continue the next day.

She continued the narration briskly. Shakuntala and her husband went to Varanasi[30] to attain moksha for their child. They went by the Chennai Varanasi Express and returned after a week. But only Swami returned. When people asked him about Shakuntala, he cried loudly and mentioned.

She went with the son, to the broad and deep Ganges. The mighty waves of Gangama[31] accepted her. She got moksha with her son. I, the great sinner am still living.

Swami found it very difficult to live in that house, where so many sweet memories were still flashing. He was basically childish in nature and he actually loves everybody in that aspect only. Shakuntala and her son were most accepted by him even though he knew the truth.

When he came out of his house, the immediate site was his son's statue. He can't control his feelings when he frequently sees them. So, he ceased to come to this house, and this house was gradually covered with thick bushes. Between bushes, we can still see the child's statue remembering the love of the couple.

Saralacca stood up from the seat as if the tale was over. She closed the front door firmly and went to the kitchen. She gave me a bottle full of drinking water and asked me to sleep.

I closed my bedroom door and tried to sleep. It was found

to be very difficult to close my eyes. When I closed my eyes, Shakuntalacca would appear on the roof which was white in color and her image was projected there from my mind.

She was well dressed in a blue embroidered net party-wear lehenga saree and its border was fashioned with peacock feather images. She had an additional ornament which was new, a nose ring with a red sparkling stone. Her necklace and bangles were the same. She smiles with charm and without any sound. She extended her carved hands to me as if calling me, to her. I even saw her tempting, deep, navel flower in between the raised hand and saree.

I jumped out of the cot and my right leg hit the table beside me. Deep pain was generated in the right leg and when I touched the particular painful area, I felt the wetness of blood and the penetration of its smell. I came to the reality and put on the light. I looked up at the sealing. The fan was rotating as usual with a little murmuring sound.

I sprayed sanitizer on the wound and pressed it to stop the bloodstream. When it was okay, I closed my eyes by sat in the chair. In the midst of the night, I was still with a dead woman, loving her and at the same time a little afraid of her.

The next day, I woke up from sleep by hearing the knock on the door. I verified the time. It was seven-thirty now. I opened the door and drank the hot tea served by Saralacca.

"How was your sleep yesterday?" Saralacca asked.

"Fine acca." I with a smile replied.

Quickly, I have finished my ablutions and prepared to go to the Cognizant. She served hot uppumavu with kadala curry. Steamed banana fruits were also provided and said these fruits were from her compound.

I bid farewell and assured her stating my revisit with family later. On the way, I was stationed before that old house and looked very closely, with eagerness.

Yes, Shakuntalacca's son was there, as a statue, in a broken mandap, looking at the travelers, silently. In due course, he will disappear into the thick bushes. Time would never fail in deeds. Anyway, I was lucky to see him, even though in a stationary form, with none to care and love. I looked again at that statue. He resembled Shakuntalacca in every sense. That wide-open eyes and keen look surely replicate the beauty queen in my adolescent days.

Shakuntalacca and her dear son, please forgive me, I was quite late to see you all.

With a heavy heart, I walked briskly to the bus stand. On, the way, near the market, there was a huge mountain of garbage. Dogs, crows, and even monkeys were searching for any food in it. In the midst of the struggle, I found a man. He was sitting behind a big waste basket and searching for food in it. He got a rotten cover of mixture and he began to eat it with delight. After finishing, he took a biscuit cover which was almost brownish in color and he pierced it, and started eating biscuits one by one.

Many pedestrians are plying on either side, but no one cares about him. I stood for a while and approached him. I opened my purse and donated a hundred rupees to him. He turned his face, looked at me, and smiled with stained teeth.

Hey, it was he, that bearded man, now grey in color. He was none other than Shakuntalacca's lover.

What a pathetic climax happened to Shakuntalacca and to her life. All my adolescent spirit which kindled my nerves was over within minutes. They escaped into thin air of truth and mocked me in revenge.

Love never fails, lust many times.

ABOUT THE AUTHOR

Presanna Kumar R

He was born and grew up in an urban area of Kottarakara in Kerala State, India. He studied B.Sc. Chemistry at Catholicate College, Pathanamthitta, and B.Ed. at Ramakrishna Institute of Moral and Spiritual Education, Mysore, in Karnataka State, India.

He was an active participant and president of various cultural forums. He wrote songs for several dramas which was staged among the public. He wrote stories in several magazines and periodicals. This is his second Kindle Direct Publishing.

His first Kindle project was "Grand Old Lady @ Rooftop Room"

After retirement, he was more concentrated on reading, writing, and in agriculture.

He is active on Blogging, Facebook, and WhatsApp.

BOOKS BY THIS AUTHOR

Grand Old Lady @ Rooftop Room

REFERENCES

1. **Ambattur** - Ambattur is located in north western part of Chennai city. This is one of 108 Shakthi Sthals in India. The Amman Temple, The Durga, here is the fifty first in the order, giving the locality the Tamil Name "aimbaththu onraam oor" meaning fifty first place or temple village which later in time transmuted as Ambattur.

2. **Kodambakkam** -K-Town or Kollywood is a business and residential neighbourhood in Central Chennai, Tamil Nadu, India. Due to the high concentration of film studios and for the status as the hub of Film industry, the name Kollywood derived.

Two theories are behind the name Kodambakkam -

a) From the Urdu word Ghoda Bagh meaning "garden of horses", of Nawab of Carnatik. His stables for numerous horses in the 17th 18th centuries supposed to serve the name.

b) From the famous snake Karkodagan of Hindu mythology. This snake worshiped Lord Siva here and there is a Siva Temple called Vengeeshwarar in Kodambakkam. In this temple several sculptures and images of the snake Karkodagan can be seen. Hence Kodambakkam derived from "Karkodagan Pakkam"

3. **COGNIZANT** - is an American multinational information technology services and consulting company. It is haedquartered in Teaneck, New Jersey, U.S. COGNIZANT is part of the NASDAQ 100 and trades under CTSH. It was founded as an in-house technology unit of Dun & Bradstreet in 1964 and started serving external clients in 1996. It had a fast growth during 2000s and became a Fortune 500 company in 2011 as of 2021, it is ranked 185.

4. **Perambalur Buddhas** - or Thiyaganur Buddha statues or Thiyganur Buddha temple are a set of historic Buddhist images

found in Thiyaganur, a village in the state of Tamil Nadu. There are two 6ft. (1.8m.) high images of Buddha in sitting posture, one of which is enshrined in a small temple and various other images scattered in the village.

The 5ft. high Buddha statue at Ogalur village has a strange story. The locals call this statue as 'The Dubai Buddha'. According to the legend, someone got a long-awaited visa to go to Dubai for a job after garlanding this Buddha statue. This incident was spread like wild fire and afterwards, devotees turned in demanding jobs in Gulf and garlanding this Buddha statue became a custom. According to them many people went to Dubai since then. The people were least bothered about Buddhism, but this statue is regularly receiving care and many garlands of Dubai aspirants, because of this legend.

5. **Coimbatore** - also spelt as Koyamputhur in Tamil, sometimes shortened as Kovai, is one of the major metropolitan cities in Tamil Nadu, India. It is located on the banks of the Noyyal River and surrounded by the Western Ghats. Coimbatore is the second largest city in Tamil Nadu. It is also called the Manchester of South India due to the presence of large scale industries, especially Textile industry.

There are two main theories behind the name Coimbatore -

a) Derivation of Kovanpudhur, meaning new town of Kovan, after the then chieftain Kovan or Koyan, and evolved into Koyamputhoor, anglicised to Coimbatore.

b) Koyamma was the name of the Goddess of Kovan. Koyamma was later evolved as Koniamma and to Kovaiamma. From Kovaiamma, the name evolved.

6. **Dr. M.G.Ramachandran** - was a film star turned politician of Tamil Nadu for a long period. He is also from Palghat, Kerala.

7. **poori and masala** - Poori or puri is a deep-fried bread made from unleavened whole-wheat flour that originated in the Indian subcontinent. It is eaten for breakfast, as a snack or light meal. The name derived from the Sanskrit word, PURIKA, or PURA means filled.

Masala curry is a combination with poori. It is actually mixture of various spices and potato chips or beetroot and made in to a paste form after cooking. It is aromatic and flavorful. Masala refers to spice blends that are added to hot oil during the curry making.

8. **maman** - uncle in Tamil, Malayalam. Here Doctor Maman means Doctor Uncle.

9. **Kilichundan mangoes** - are medium size with greenish yellow in nature. The skin is green when unripe and turns golden-yellow. Mango has unique flavor that is a combination of sweetness and tanginess.

Kilichundan means the beak of a bird in Malayalam, the language of Kerala state, India. It is used to make pickles and curries.

10.**Sivaji Ganesan** - is his stage name. Real name is Villupuram Chinnaiya Manrayar Ganesamoorthy. (1928 - 2001) He is acknowledged as one of the greatest Indian actors of all time. For his versatile and variety roles in films, he was nicknamed 'Nadikar Thilagam', meaning - the pride of actors. He exhibited the ability to remember lengthy lines easily and this favoured lead roles in dramas. His portrayal of Shivaji in the stage play Shivaji Kanda Hindu Rajyam earned him the monicker "Sivaji". He played lead role in over 250 films, a record in Tamil film industry.

11. **T.M. Soundararajan** - Thoguluva Meenatchi Iyengar Soundararajan, popularly known as TMS, was an Indian Carnatic musician and a playback singer for over six and a half decades. (1923 - 2013) He was born in Madurai, Tamil Nadu, India. He lent his voice to almost all actors of old and new generation film artists. He was in the field up to the age of 88.

12. **Damocles sword** - dates back to ancient moral parable of Roman philosopher Cicero in his book 'Tusculan Disputations'. His tale centers on a tyrannical king Dionysius. He was powerful, rich and cruel, so had many enemies. He was tormented by fears of assassination, so slept in a bedchamber surrounded by a moat and only trusted his daughters to shave his beard with a razor.

Damocles, a court flatterer once showered the King with compliments and remarked how blissful his life must be. After hearing this the King Dionyius replied in annoyance, "do you wish to taste it yourself and make a trial of good fortune?

Damocles agreed, he was seated on a golden couch, ordered a host of servants and treated to succulent cuts of meat and lavished with scented perfumes and ointments.

Thinking his luck and just as he was starting to enjoy the life of a King, he noticed that Dionysius had also hung a razor-sharp sword just ponting his head, suspended only by a single horsehair. He became nervous and asked the King for excuse.

The idea behind the tale is those in power always labor under the specter of anxiety and death, and "there can be no happiness for one who is under constant apprehensions"

13. **mallika flowers** - Mallika, Jasmine flower (chameli -mulla or malligai), several species of which are native to India, is fragrant flower and is widely used in the worship of Gods and Goddesses in Hinduism. Garlands made of jasmine flowers are offered to deities in temples and also in Hindu homes as part of daily worship.

Indian women especially of South India adorned their hair with jasmine flowers or garlands made up of it.

14. **Hanuman Temple** - Hanuman also called Maruti, Bjrangabali, Anjaneya is a Hindu God and a divine vanara (monkey) companion of the God Sri Rama. Hanuman is one of the central characters of Hindu epic Ramayana. Hanuman is considered as Vayuputra, the son of wind-god Vayu, who is one of the chiranjivis.(Immortal) Hanuman is mentioned in several other Hindu texts such as Mahabharata, and various Puranas.

15. **Translation from Tamil dialogue** - 'Athul, why are you not eating meat? Both of you have brought it from the market in the morning. Eat it full.'

16. **Moore Market** - was originally built to house the hawkers in the Broadway area of Madras. Its foundation stone was laid by Sir. Gorge Moore, President of the Madras corporation in 1898. The market, which consisted a series of shops around a central quadrangle and had sections of meat, flowers, food items, antiques, art, books, pets, rare and second hand items for a bargain.

On 30 May 1985, the old building was destroyed for expanding the MGR Chennai Central Railway station.

Marina Beach - or **Marina** is a natural urban beach in Chennai, Tamil Nadu, India, along the Bay of Bengal. The beach runs from near Fort St. George in the North to Foreshore Estate in the South. a distance of 6.0 kilometer making the second longest urban beach in the world.

Zoo and Museum - Arignar Anna Zoological Park also known as Vanadalur Zoo, located at Vandalur, Chennai, Tamil Nadu, India.Established in 1855, it is the first public zoo in India. Spread over an area of 602 hectares, the park is the largest zoological park in India.

The Madras museum is a museum of human history and culture located in the Government Museum Complex in the neighbourhood of Egmore in Chennai, India. Started in 1851, it is the second oldest museum in India.

17. AVM studio - is an Indian film production studio founded by A.V. Meiyappan. It is the oldest studio in India, located in Vadapalani, Chennai, India. It has produced more than 300 films in various South Indian languages.

18.Saibaba of Shirdi - was an Indian spiritual master and fakir who is considered to be a saint and revered by both Hindu and Muslim devotees. He preached the importance of 'realization of the self' and criticized 'love towards perishable things'. His teachings focused on a moral code of love, forgiveness, helping others, charity, contentment, inner peace and devotion to God and Guru.

Shirdi is worshipped by people around the world.

19. Triplicane - is the anglicized version of *Thiruvallikeni*, which derives from *Thiru-Alli-Keni* (Sacred Lily Pond in Tamil), denoting the pond in front of Parthasarathy Temple. {Lord Sri Krishna Temple}

Triplicane is the oldest neighbourhoods of Chennai, India. It is situated on the Bay of Bengal coast and about 0.6 kilometer from Fort St.George.

20. Translation from Tamil dialogue -
'Which are the places you visited so far in chennai?'

21. Translation from Tamil dialogue -

'Have you visited Asoka Park at Triplicane?'
22. Translation from Tamil dialogue -
'I had seen you, in that park with Grandpa, Kanna."
23. Translation from Tamil dialogue
'Athul you're just like a brother to me'
24. Translation from Tamil dialogue
'Study well and remember me.'
25. Translation from Tamil dialogue
'Nee en thambi..nee en thambi.'
26. LIC - Life Insurance Corporation of India, public sector company headquartered in Mumbai, India. It is the largest insurance company in India, established on 1 september 1956.
27. Mount Road -is the former name, now it is Anna Salai, is an arterial road in chennai, India. It starts at the Cooum Creek, south of Fort St. George, leading in a south-westerly direction towards St.Thomas Mount and ends at the Kathipara Junction.
28. Kilpauk Medical College - Founded in 1960, is a Government medical College. Actually, the college has a long back history from 1925. it was then started as offering L IM. Now it is a full-fledged college offering most modern health care and courses.
29. sandhya vandhanam - is the salutation to (Goddess) Twilight or salutation during the twilight is a mandatory religious ritual centring around the recitation of the Gayatri Mantra. The Sandhyavandhanam consists of ritual recitation from the Vedas, three times a day- at morning (pratassandhya), at noon (madhyahnika) and evening (sayamsamdhya).
The Gayatri mantra -
"Om bhur bhuvah suvah
tat savitur varenyam
bhrgo devasya dhimahi
dhiyo yo nah pracodayat"
- Rigveda 3.62.10
Meaning - 'O thou existence Absolute, Creator of the three dimensions, we contemplate upon thy divine light'.
30. Varanasi - also Banaras or Benares or simply Kashi is Holy City of the Hindus. It is on the bank of Ganges River in Northern India

that has a central place in the traditions of pilgrimage, death and Moksha.

Varanasi is one of the world's oldest continually inhabited city.

31. Gangama - River Ganges is called by Hindus as Gangama, meaning Mother Ganga. Ganga is considered as sacred and a dip in this river is considered as Papamoksha, forgiveness from all sins committed. A death in this river is considered moksha and attainment of heavenly abode.

ACKNOWLEDGEMENT

* Wikipedia, the online Encyclopedia, for various Reference materials.

Made in the USA
Columbia, SC
17 September 2023

22918139R00033